Praise for *Inside Out & Back Again*

Winner of the National Book Award
for Young People's Literature
A Newbery Honor Book
A #1 *New York Times* Bestseller
An ALA Notable Book
A *Publishers Weekly* Flying Start
A Book Links Lasting Connection Book

"Based in Lại's personal experience, this novel captures a child-refugee's struggle, with rare honesty. Written in accessible, short free-verse poems, Hà's immediate narrative describes her mistakes—both humorous and heartbreaking; and readers will be moved by Hà's sorrow as they recognize the anguish of being the outcast."   —ALA *Booklist* (starred review)

"An enlightening, poignant, and unexpectedly funny novel in verse. In her not-to-be-missed debut, Lại evokes a distinct time and place and presents a complex, realistic heroine whom readers will recognize, even if they haven't found themselves in a strange new country."   —*Kirkus Reviews* (starred review)

"The taut portrayal of Hà's emotional life is especially poignant as she cycles from feeling smart in Vietnam to struggling in the States, and finally regains academic and social confidence. An incisive portrait of human resilience."

—*Publishers Weekly* (starred review)

"Hà's voice is full of humor and hope."

"In this free-verse narrative, Lại is sparing in her details, painting big pictures with few words and evoking abundant visuals."

Inside
Out
&
Back
Again

THANHHÀ LẠI

HARPER
An Imprint of HarperCollinsPublishers

Library of Congress Cataloging-in-Publication Data

Lại, Thanhhà.

Inside out and back again / Thanhhà Lại. — 1st ed.

p. cm.

Summary: Through a series of poems, a young girl chronicles the
life-changing year of 1975, when she, her mother, and her brothers
leave Vietnam and resettle in Alabama.

ISBN 978-0-06-257402-2

[1. Novels in verse. 2. Vietnamese Americans—Fiction.
3. Emigration and immigration—Fiction. 4. Immigrants—
Fiction. 5. Vietnam—History—1971–1980—Fiction.
6. Alabama—History—1951—Fiction.] I. Title.

PZ7.5.L35In 2011   2010007855
[Fic]—dc22   CIP
                                                          AC

Typography by Ray Shappell

19 20 21 PC/LSCH 10 9 8 7 6 5 4 3 2

❖

Harper Classic edition, 2017

To the millions of refugees in the world,
may you each find a home

PART I

Saigon

1975: *Year of the Cat*

Today is Tết,
the first day
of the lunar calendar.

Every Tết
we eat sugary lotus seeds
and glutinous rice cakes.
We wear all new clothes,
even underneath.

Mother warns
how we act today
foretells the whole year.

Everyone must smile
no matter how we feel.

No one can sweep,
for why sweep away hope?
No one can splash water,
for why splash away joy?

Today
we all gain one year in age,
no matter the date we were born.
Tết, our New Year's,
doubles as everyone's birthday.

Now I am ten, learning
to embroider circular stitches,
to calculate fractions into percentages,
to nurse my papaya tree to bear many fruits.

But last night I pouted
when Mother insisted
one of my brothers
must rise first
this morning
to bless our house
because only male feet
can bring luck.

An old, angry knot
expanded in my throat.

I decided
to wake before dawn
and tap my big toe

to the tile floor
first.

Not even Mother,
sleeping beside me, knew.

February 11
Tết

Inside Out

Every new year Mother visits
the I Ching Teller of Fate.
This year he predicts
our lives will twist inside out.

Maybe soldiers will no longer
patrol our neighborhood,
maybe I can jump rope
after dark,
maybe the whistles
that tell Mother
to push us under the bed
will stop screeching.

But I heard
on the playground
this year's *bánh chưng*,
eaten only during Tết,
will be smeared in blood.

The war is coming
closer to home.

February 12

Kim Hà

My name is Hà.

Brother Quang remembers
I was as red and fat
as a baby hippopotamus
when he first saw me,
inspiring the name
Hà Mã,
River Horse.

Brother Vũ screams, *Hà Ya*,
and makes me jump
every time
he breaks wood or bricks
in imitation of Bruce Lee.

Brother Khôi calls me
Mother's Tail
because I'm always
three steps from her.

I can't make my brothers
go live elsewhere,
but I can
hide their sandals.

We each have but one pair,
much needed
during this dry season
when the earth stings.

Mother tells me
to ignore my brothers.
We named you Kim Hà,
after the Golden (Kim) *River* (Hà),
where Father and I
once strolled in the evenings.

My parents had no idea
what three older brothers
can do
to the simple name
Hà.

Mother tells me,
They tease you
because they adore you.

She's wrong,
but I still love
being near her, even more than I love

my papaya tree.
I will offer her
its first fruit.

Every day

Papaya Tree

It grew from a seed
I flicked into
the back garden.

A seed like
a fish eye,
slippery
shiny
black.

The tree has grown
twice as tall
as I stand
on tippy toes.

Brother Khôi spotted
the first white blossom.
Four years older,
he can see higher.

Brother Vũ later found
a baby papaya
the size of a fist
clinging to the trunk.

At eighteen,
he can see that much higher.

Brother Quang is oldest,
twenty-one and studying engineering.
Who knows what he will notice
before me?

I vow
to rise first every morning
to stare at the dew
on the green fruit
shaped like a lightbulb.

I will be the first
to witness its ripening.

Mid-February

TiTi Waves Good-bye

My best friend TiTi
is crying hard,
snotting the hem
of her pink fluffy blouse.

Her two brothers
also are sniffling
inside their car
packed to the roof
with suitcases.

TiTi shoves into my hand
a tin of flower seeds
we gathered last fall.
We hoped to plant them
together.

She waves from the back window
of their rabbit-shaped car.
Her tears mix with long strands of hair,
long hair I wish I had.

I would still be standing there
crying and waving to nothing

if Brother Khôi hadn't come
to take my hand.

They're heading to Vũng Tầu,
he says,
where the rich go
to flee Vietnam
on cruise ships.

I'm glad we've become poor
so we can stay.

Early March

Missing in Action

Father left home
on a navy mission
on this day
nine years ago
when I was almost one.

He was captured
on Route 1
an hour south of the city
by moped.

That's all we know.

This day
Mother prepares an altar
to chant for his return,
offering fruit,
incense,
tuberoses,
and glutinous rice.

She displays his portrait
taken during Tết
the year he disappeared.

How peaceful he looks,
smiling,
peacock tails
at the corners
of his eyes.

Each of us bows
and wishes
and hopes
and prays.

Everything on the altar
remains for the day
except the portrait.
Mother locks it away
as soon as her chant ends.

She cannot bear
to look into Father's
forever-young
eyes.

March 10

Mother's Days

On weekdays
Mother's a secretary
in a navy office,
trusted to count out
salaries in cash
at the end of each month.

At night
she stays up late
designing and cutting
baby clothes
to give to seamstresses.

A few years ago
she made enough money
to consider
buying a car.

On weekends
she takes me to market stalls,
dropping off the clothes
and trying to collect
on last week's goods.

Hardly anyone buys anymore,
she says.
People can barely afford food.

Still,
she continues to try.

March 15

Eggs

Brother Khôi
is mad at Mother
for taking his hen's
eggs.

The hen gives
one egg
every day and a half.

We take turns
eating them.

Brother Khôi
refuses to eat his,
putting each under a lamp
in hopes of
a chick.

I should side with
my most tolerable brother,
but I love a soft yolk
to dip bread.

Mother says
if the price of eggs

were not the price of rice,
and the price of rice
were not the price of gasoline,
and the price of gasoline
were not the price of gold,
then of course
Brother Khôi
could continue hatching eggs.

She's sorry.

March 17

Current News

Every Friday
in Miss Xinh's class
we talk about
current news.

But when we keep talking about
how close the Communists
have gotten to Saigon,
how much prices have gone up
since American soldiers left,
how many distant bombs
were heard the previous night,
Miss Xinh finally says no more.

From now on
Fridays
will be for
happy news.

No one has anything
to say.

March 21

Feel Smart

This year
I have afternoon classes,
plus Saturdays.
We attend in shifts
so everyone can fit
into school.

Mornings free,
Mother trusts me
to shop at the open market.

Last September
she would give me
fifty đồng
to buy one hundred grams of pork,
a bushel of water spinach,
five cubes of tofu.

But I told no one
I was buying
ninety-nine grams of pork,
seven-eighths of a bushel of spinach,
four and three-quarter cubes of tofu.
Merchants frowned at
Mother's strange instructions.

The money saved
bought
a pouch of toasted coconut,
one sugary fried dough,
two crunchy mung bean cookies.

Now it takes two hundred đồng
to buy the same things.

I still buy less pork,
allowing myself just the fried dough.

No one knows
and I feel smart.

Late March

Two More Papayas

I see them first.

Two green thumbs
that will grow into
orange-yellow delights
smelling of summer.

Middle sweet
between a mango and a pear.

Soft as a yam
gliding down
after three easy,
thrilling chews.

April 5

Unknown Father

I don't know
any more about Father
than the small things
Mother lets slip.

He loved stewed eels,
paté chaud pastries,
and of course his children,
so much that he
grew teary
watching us sleep.

He hated the afternoon sun,
the color brown,
and cold rice.

Brother Quang remembers
Father often said
tuyết sút,
the Vietnamese way
to pronounce the French phrase
tout de suite
meaning *right away.*

Mother would laugh

when Father followed her
around the kitchen
repeating,
I'm starved for stewed eel,
tuyết sút, tuyết sút.

Sometimes I whisper
tuyết sút to myself
to pretend
I know him.

I would never say *tuyết sút*
in front of Mother.
None of us would want
to make her sadder
than she already is.

Every day

TV News

Brother Quang races home
from class,
throws down his bicycle,
exhausted,
no longer able to afford
gasoline for his moped.

Unbelievable,
he screams,
and turns on the TV.

A pilot for South Vietnam
bombed the presidential palace
downtown that afternoon.
Afterward the pilot flew north
and received a medal.

The news says the pilot
has been a spy
for the Communists
for years.

The Communists
captured Father,
so why would

any pilot
choose their side?

Brother Quang says,
One cannot justify war
unless each side
flaunts its own
blind conviction.

Since starting college,
he shows off even more
with tangled words.

I start to say so,
but Mother pats my hand,
her signal for me to calm down.

April 8

Birthday

I, the youngest,
get to celebrate
my actual birthday
even though I turned
a year older
like everyone else
at Tết.

I, the only daughter,
usually get roasted chicken,
dried bamboo soup,
and all-I-can-eat pudding.

This year,
Mother manages only
banana tapioca
and my favorite
black sesame candy.

She makes up for it
by allowing
one wish.

I dye my mouth

sugary black
and insist on
stories.

It's not easy
to persuade Mother
to tell of her girlhood
in the North,
where her grandmother's land
stretched farther than
doves could fly,
where looking pretty
and writing poetry
were her only duties.

She was promised to Father
at five.
They married at sixteen,
earlier than expected.
Everyone's future changed
upon learning the name
Hồ Chí Minh.

Change meant
land was taken away,
houses now belonged

to the state,
servants gained power
as fighters.

The country divided in half.

Mother and Father came south,
convinced it would be
easier to breathe
away from Communism.

Her father was to follow,
but he was waiting for his son,
who was waiting for his wife,
who was waiting to deliver a child
in its last week
in her belly.

The same week,
North and South
closed their doors.
No more migration.
No more letters.
No more family.

At this point,
Mother closes her eyes,

eyes that resemble no one else's,
sunken and deep like Westerners'
yet almond-shaped like ours.
I always wish for her eyes,
but Mother says no.
Eyes like hers can't help
but carry sadness;
even as a child
her parents were alarmed
by the weight in her eyes.

I want to hear more,
but nothing,
not even my pouts,
can make Mother open her eyes
and tell more.

April 10

Birthday Wishes

Wishes I keep to myself:

Wish I could do what boys do
and let the sun darken my skin,
and scars grid my knees.

Wish I could let my hair grow,
but Mother says the shorter the better
to beat Saigon's heat and lice.

Wish I could lose my chubby cheeks.

Wish I could stay calm
no matter what
my brothers say.

Wish Mother would stop
chiding me to stay calm,
which makes it worse.

Wish I had a sister
to jump rope with
and sew doll clothes
and hug for warmth
in the middle of the night.

Wish Father would come home
so I can stop daydreaming
that he will appear
in my classroom
in a white navy uniform
and extend his hand toward me
for all my classmates to see.

Mostly I wish
Father would appear in our doorway
and make Mother's lips
curl upward,
lifting them from
a permanent frown
of worries.

April 10
Night

A Day Downtown

Every spring
President Thiệu
holds a long long long
ceremony to comfort
war wives.

Mother and I go because
after President Thiệu's
talk talk talk—
of winning the war,
of democracy,
of our fathers' bravery—
each family gets
five kilos of sugar,
ten kilos of rice,
and a small jug of
vegetable oil.

Inside the cyclo
Mother crosses her legs
so I can fit beside her.
The breeze still cool,
we bounce across the bridge
shaped like a crescent moon
where I'm not to go by myself.

Mother smells of lavender
and warmth;
she's so beautiful
even if
her cheeks are too hollow,
her mouth too dark with worries.
Despite warnings,
I still want her sunken eyes.

Before I see it,
I hear downtown,
thick with beeps,
shouts, police whistles.
Everywhere,
mopeds and bicycles
race down the wide road,
moving out of the way
only when a truck
honks and mows straight down
the middle of the lane.

We get out
in front of an open market.
We push our way to
a *bánh cuốn* stand.
I love watching

the spread of rice flour on cloth,
stretched over a steaming pot.
Like magic a crepe forms
to be filled with shrimp
and eaten with
cucumber and bean sprouts.

It tastes even better
than it looks.
While my mouth is full,
the noises of the market
silence themselves,
letting me and my *bánh cuốn*
float.

We squeeze ourselves
out of the market,
toward the presidential palace.

We stand in line;
for even longer
we sit on hot metal benches
facing the podium.

My white cotton hat
and Mother's flowery umbrella

are nothing
against the afternoon sun,
shooting rays into
my short short hair.

I'm dizzy
and thirsty;
the fish sauce
in the *bánh cuốn*
was very salty.

Mother gives me a tamarind candy.
I have never been
so thrilled
to drink my saliva.

Finally President Thiệu appears,
tan and sweaty.
We know you have suffered.
I thank you,
your country thanks you.

Then he cries actual tears,
unwiped, facing the cameras.

Mother clicks her tongue:

Tears of an ugly fish.

I know that to mean
fake tears of a crocodile.

April 12

Twisting Twisting

Mother measures
rice grains
left in the bin.
Not enough to last
till payday
at the end of the month.

Her brows
twist like laundry
being wrung dry.

Yam and manioc
taste lovely
blended with rice,
she says, and smiles,
as if I don't know
how the poor
fill their children's bellies.

April 13

Closed Too Soon

A siren screams
over Miss Xinh's voice
in the middle of a lesson
on smiley and bald
President Ford.

We all know it's bad news.

School's now closed;
everyone must go home
a month too soon.

I'm mad and pinch the girl
who shares my desk.
Tram is half my size,
so skinny and nervous.

Our mothers are friends.
She will tell on me.
She always tells on me.

Mother will again
scold me to be gentle.

I need time
to finish this riddle:
A man usually rides his bike
9 kilometers per hour,
yet the wind slows him
to 6.76 kilometers
for 26 minutes
and 5.55 kilometers
for 10;
how long until he gets home
11.54 kilometers away?

The first to solve it
gets the sweet potato plant
sprouting at the window.
I want to plant it
beside my papaya tree,
where vines can climb
and shade ripening fruit.

Again I pinch Tram,
knowing the plant
will be awarded
today
to the teacher's pet,

who is always
skinny and nervous
and never me.

April 14

Promises

Five papayas
the sizes of
my head,
a knee,
two elbows,
and a thumb
cling to the trunk.

Still green
but promising.

April 15

Bridge to the Sea

Uncle Sơn,
Father's best friend,
visits us.

He's short, dark, and smiley,
not tall, thin, and serious
like Father in photographs.
Still, when classmates
ask about my father,
sometimes short and smiley
come to mind
before I can stop it.

Uncle Sơn goes straight
to the kitchen,
where the back door opens into
an alley.
Unbelievable luck!
This door bypasses the navy checkpoint
and leads straight to the port.

I will not risk
fleeing with my children
on a rickety boat.

Would a navy ship
meet your approval?

    As if the navy
    would abandon its country?

There won't be a South Vietnam
left to abandon.

    You really believe
    we can leave?

When the time comes,
this house
is our bridge
to the sea.

                                      April 16

Should We?

Mother calls a family meeting.

Ông Xuân has sold
leaves of gold
to buy twelve airplane tickets.

Bà Nam has a van
ready to load
twenty-five relatives
toward the coast.

Mother asks us,
Should we leave our home?

Brother Quang says,
How can we scramble away
like rats,
without honor, without dignity,
when everyone must help
rebuild the country?

Brother Khôi says,
What if Father comes home
and finds his family gone?

Brother Vũ says,
Yes, we must go.

Everyone knows he dreams
of touching the same ground
where Bruce Lee walked.

Mother twists her brows.
I've lived in the North.
At first, not much will happen,
then suddenly Quang
will be asked to leave college.
Hà will come home
chanting the slogans
of Hồ Chí Minh,
and Khôi will be rewarded
for reporting to his teacher
everything we say in the house.

Her brows twist
so much
we hush.

April 17

Sssshhhhhh

Brother Khôi shakes me
before dawn.

I follow him
to the back garden.
In his palm chirps
a downy yellow fuzz,
just hatched.

He presses his palm
against my squeal.

No matter what Mother decides,
we are not to leave.
I must protect my chick
and you your papayas.

He holds out his pinky
and stares
stares
stares
until I extend mine
and we hook.

April 18

Quiet Decision

Dinnertime
I help Mother
peel sweet potatoes
to stretch the rice.

I start to chop off
a potato's end
as wide as
a thumbnail,
then decide
to slice off
only a sliver.

I am proud
of my ability
to save
until I see
tears
in Mother's
deep eyes.

You deserve to grow up
where you don't worry about
saving half a bite
of sweet potato.

April 19

Early Monsoon

We pretend
the monsoon
has come early.

In the distance
bombs
explode like thunder,
slashes
lighten the sky,
gunfire
falls like rain.

Distant
yet within ears,
within eyes.

Not that far away
after all.

April 20

The President Resigns

On TV President Thiệu
looks sad and yellow;
what has happened to his tan?

His eyes brim with tears;
this time they look real.
I can no longer be your president
but I will never leave my people
or our country.

Mother lifts one brow,
what she does
when she thinks
I'm lying.

April 21

Watch Over Us

Uncle Sơn returns
and tells us
to be ready to leave
any day.

Don't tell anyone,
or all of Saigon
will storm the port.
Only navy families
can board the ships.

Uncle Sơn and Father
graduated in the same navy class.
It was mere luck
that Uncle Sơn
didn't go on the mission
where Father was captured.

Mother pulls me close
and pats my head.
Father watches over us
even if he's not here.

Mother tells me
she and Father have a pact.

If war should separate them,
they know to find each other
through Father's ancestral home
in the North.

April 24

Crisscrossed Packs

Pedal, pedal
Mother's feet
push the sewing machine.
The faster she pedals
the faster stitches appear
on heavy brown cloth.

Two rectangles
make a pack.
A long strip
makes a handle
to be strapped across
the wearer's chest.

Hours later
the stitches appear
in slow motion,
the needle a worm
laying tiny eggs
that sink into brown cloth.
The tired worm
reproduces much more slowly
at the end of the day
than at the beginning
when Mother started

the first of five bags.

Brother Khôi says too loudly,
Make only three.

Mother goes
to a high shelf,
bringing back Father's portrait.

Come with us
or we'll all stay.
Think, my son;
your action will determine
our future.

Mother knows this son
cannot stand to hurt
anyone,
anything.

Look at Father.
Come with us
so Father
will be proud
you obeyed your mother
while he's not here.

I look at my toes,
feeling Brother Khôi's eyes
burn into my scalp.

I also feel him slowly nodding.

Who can go against
a mother
who has become gaunt like bark
from raising four children alone?

April 26

Choice

Into each pack:
one pair of pants,
one pair of shorts,
three pairs of underwear,
two shirts,
sandals,
toothbrush and paste,
soap,
ten palms of rice grains,
three clumps of cooked rice,
one choice.

I choose my doll,
once lent to a neighbor
who left it outside,
where mice bit
her left cheek
and right thumb.

I love her more
for her scars.

I dress her
in a red and white dress
with matching hat and booties
that Mother knitted.

April 27

Left Behind

Ten gold-rimmed glasses
Father brought back from America
where he trained before I was born.

Brother Quang's
report cards,
each ranking him first in class,
beginning in kindergarten.

Vines of bougainvillea
fully in bloom,
burgundy and white
like the colors
of our house.

Vines of jasmine
in front of every window
that remind Mother
of the North.

A cowboy leather belt
Brother Vũ sewed
on Mother's machine

and broke her needle.
That was when
he adored
Johnny Cash
more than
Bruce Lee.

A row of glass jars
Brother Khôi used
to raise fighting fish.

Two hooks
and the hammock
where I nap.

Photographs:
every Tết at the zoo,
Father in his youth,
Mother in her youth,
baby pictures,
where you can't tell whose bottom
is exposed for all the world to see.

Mother chooses ten
and burns the rest.

We cannot leave
evidence of Father's life
that might hurt him.

April 27
Evening

Wet and Crying

My biggest papaya
is light yellow,
still flecked with green.

Brother Vũ wants
to cut it down,
saying it's better than
letting the Communists have it.

Mother says yellow papaya
tastes lovely
dipped in chili salt.
*You children should eat
fresh fruit
while you can.*

Brother Vũ chops;
the head falls;
a silver blade slices.

Black seeds spill
like clusters of eyes,
wet and crying.

April 28

Sour Backs

At the port
we find out
there's no such thing
as a secret
among the Vietnamese.

Thousands
found out
about the navy ships
ready to abandon the navy.

Uncle Sơn flares elbows into wings,
lunges forward
protecting his children.

But our family sticks together
like wet pages.
I see nothing but backs
sour and sweaty.

Brother Vũ steps up,
placing Mother in front of him
and lifting me
onto his shoulders.

His palms press
Brothers Quang and Khôi
forward.

I promise myself
to never again
make fun of
Bruce Lee.

April 29
Afternoon

One Mat Each

We climb on
and claim a space
of two straw mats
under the deck,
enough for us five
to lie side by side.

By sunset our space
is one straw mat,
enough for us five
to huddle together.

Bodies cram
every centimeter
below deck,
then every centimeter
on deck.

Everyone knows the ship
could sink,
unable to hold
the piles of bodies
that keep crawling on
like raging ants
from a disrupted nest.

But no one
is heartless enough
to say
stop
because what if
they had been
stopped
before their turn?

April 29
Sunset

In the Dark

Uncle Sơn visits
and whispers to Mother.

We follow Mother
who follows Uncle Sơn
who leads his family
up to the deck
and off the ship.

It has been said
the ship next door
has a better engine,
more water,
endless fuel,
countless salty eggs.

Uncle Sơn lingers
without getting on
the new ship;
so do we.

Hordes pour
by us,
beyond us.

Above us
bombs pierce the sky.
Red and green flares
explode like fireworks.

All lights are off
so the port will not be
a target.

In the dark
a nudge here
a nudge there
and we end up
back on the first ship
in the same spot
with two mats.

Without lights
our ship glides out to sea,
emptied of half its passengers.

April 29
Near midnight

Saigon Is Gone

I listen to
the swish, swish
of Mother's handheld fan,
the whispers among adults,
the bombs in the ever greater distance.

The commander has ordered
everyone below deck
even though he has chosen
a safe river route
to connect to the sea,
avoiding the obvious escape path
through Vũng Tầu,
where the Communists are dropping
all the bombs they have left.

I hope TiTi got out.

Mother is sick
with waves in her stomach
even though the ship
barely creeps along.

We hear a helicopter
circling circling

near our ship.

People run and scream,
Communists!

Our ship dips low
as the crowd runs to the left,
and then to the right.

This is not helping Mother.

I wish they would stand still
and hush.

The commander is talking:
Do not be frightened!
It's a pilot for our side
who has jumped into the water,
letting his helicopter
plunge in behind him.

The pilot
appears below deck,
wet and shaking.

He salutes the commander
and shouts,

At noon today the Communists
crashed their tanks
through the gates
of the presidential palace
and planted on the roof
a flag with one huge star.

Then he adds
what no one wants to hear:
It's over;
Saigon is gone.

April 30
Late afternoon

PART II

At Sea

Floating

Our ship creeps along
the river route
without lights
without cooking
without bathrooms.

We are told
to sip water
only when we must
so our bodies
can stop needing.

Mine won't listen.

Mother sighs.

I don't blame her,
having a daughter
who's either
dying of thirst
or demanding release.

Other girls
must be made
of bamboo,

bending whichever way
they are told.

Mother tells Uncle Sơn
I need a bathroom.

We are allowed
into the commander's cabin,
where the bathroom is
so white and clean,
so worth the embarrassment.

May 1

S-l-o-w-l-y

I nibble on
the last clump
of cooked rice
from my sack.

Hard and moldy,
yet chewy and sweet
inside.

I chew each grain
s-l-o-w-l-y.

I hear others chew
but have never seen
anyone actually eating.

No one has offered
to share
what I smell:
sardines, dried durian,
salted eggs, toasted sesame.
I lean toward
the family
on the next mat.

Mother firmly
shakes her head.
She looks so sad
as she pats
my hand.

May 2

Rations

On the third day
we join the sea
toward Thailand.

The commander says
it's safe enough
for his men to cook,
for us to go above deck,
for all to smile a little.

He says there's enough
rice and water
for three weeks,
but rescue should happen
much earlier.

Do not worry,
ships from all countries
are out looking for us.

Morning, noon, and night
we each get
one clump of rice,
small, medium, large,
according to our height,

plus one cup of water
no matter our size.

The first hot bite
of freshly cooked rice,
plump and nutty,
makes me imagine
the taste of ripe papaya
although one has nothing
to do with the other.

May 3

Routine

Mother cannot allow
idle children,
hers or anyone else's.

After one week
on the ship
Brother Quang begins
English lessons.

I wish he would
keep it to:
How are you?
This is a pen.
But when an adult is not there
he says,
We must consider the shame
of abandoning our own country
and begging toward the unknown
where we will all begin again
at the lowest level
on the social scale.

It's better in the afternoons
with Brother Vũ,
who just wants us

to do front kicks
and back kicks,
at times adding
one-two punches.

Brother Khôi gets to monitor
lines for the bathrooms,
where bottoms stick out
to the sea
behind blankets blowing
in the wind.

When not in class
I have to stay
within sight of Mother,
like a baby.

Mother gives me
her writing pad.
Write tiny,
there's but one pad.

Writing becomes
boring,
so I draw
over my words.

Pouches of pan-fried shredded coconut
Tamarind paste on banana leaf
Steamed corn on the cob
Rounds of fried dough
Wedges of pineapple on a stick
And of course
cubes of papaya tender and shiny.

Mother smoothes back my hair,
knowing the pain
of a girl
who loves snacks
but is stranded
on a ship.

May 7

Once Knew

Water, water, water
everywhere
making me think
land is just something
I once knew
like

napping on a hammock

bathing without salt

watching Mother write

laughing for no reason

kicking up powdery dirt

and

wearing clean nightclothes
smelling of the sun.

May 12

Brother Khôi's Secret

Brother Khôi stinks;
we can't ignore it.

He stews and sweats
in a jacket
he won't take off.

Forced to sponge-wipe
twice a day,
he wraps the jacket
around his waist.

He keeps clutching something
in the left pocket,
where the stench grows.

Neighbors complain,
even the ones
eight mats away,
saying it's bad enough
being trapped
in putrid, hot air
made from fermented bodies
and oily sweat,
must everybody

also endure
something rotten?

Finally Brother Vũ
holds Brother Khôi down
and forces him
to open his hand.

A flattened chick
lies crooked,
neck dangling
off his palm.

The chick had not
a chance
after we shoved
for hours to board.

Brother Khôi screams,
kicks everything off our mats.
Brother Quang
carries him
above deck.

Quiet.

May 13

Last Respects

After two weeks at sea
the commander calls
all of us above deck
for a formal lowering of
our yellow flag
with three red stripes.

South Vietnam no longer exists.

One woman tries to throw
herself overboard,
screaming that without a country
she cannot live.
As they wrestle her down,
a man stabs his heart
with a toothbrush.

I don't know them,
so their pain seems unreal
next to Brother Khôi's,
whose eyes are as wild
as those of his broken chick.

I hold his hand:
Come with me.

He doesn't resist.

Alone
at the back of the ship
I open Mother's white handkerchief.
Inside lies my mouse-bitten doll,
her arms wrapped around
the limp fuzzy body of his chick.

I tie it all into a bundle.

Brother Khôi nods
and I smile,
but I regret
not having my doll
as soon as the white bundle
sinks into the sea.

May 14

One Engine

In the middle
of the night
our ship stops.

Mother hugs me,
hearts drumming
as one.

If the Communists
catch us fleeing,
it's a million times worse
than staying at home.

After many shouts
and much time
the ship moves forward
with just one engine.

Mother would not
release me.

The commander says,
Thailand is much farther
on one engine.
It was risky to take

the river route.
We escaped bombs
but missed the rescue ships.

The commander decides
the ration is now
half a clump of rice
only at morning and night,
and one cup of water
all day.

Sip,
he says,
and don't waste strength
moving around
because it's impossible
to predict
how much longer
we will
be floating.

May 16

The Moon

During the day
the deck belongs
to men and children.

At nightfall
women make their way
up.

In single files
they sponge-bathe
and relieve themselves
behind blanket curtains.

I always stand in line
with Mother.

Every night
she points upward.
*At least
the moon remains
unchanged.*

*Your father could be looking
at the same round moon.
He may already understand*

we will wait for him
across the world.

I feel guilty,
having not once
thought of Father.

I can't wish for him
to appear
until I know where
we'll be.

May 18

A Kiss

The horn on our ship
blows and blows,
waking everyone
from a week-long nap.

A sure answer,
honk honk,
seems close enough
and real enough
to call everyone on deck.

A gigantic ship
with an American flag
moves closer.
Men in white uniform
wave and smile.

Our commander wears
his navy jacket and hat,
so white and so crisp.

Now I realize
why I like him so much.
In uniform,
he looks just like Father.

He boards the other ship,
salutes and shakes hands
with a man whose hair
grows on his face
not on his head
in the color of flames.

I had not known
such hair was possible.

We clap and clap
as the ships draw together
and kiss.

Boxes and boxes
pass onto our deck.
Oranges, apples, bananas,
cold sweet bubbly drinks,
chocolate drops, fruity gum.

The American ship
tows ours
with a steel braid
thick as my body.

Our rescue now certain,
the party blossoms
as food suddenly
comes up from below.
Ramen noodles, beef jerky,
dried shrimp, butter biscuits,
tamarind pods, canned fish,
and drums and drums of real water.

Mother says,
People share
when they know
they have escaped hunger.

Shouldn't people share
because there is hunger?

That night I stand behind
blowing blankets
and pour fresh water
all over my skin.

How sweet water tastes
even when mixed with soap.

May 24

93

Golden Fuzz

Water, water
still everywhere
but in the distance
appears a black dot.

We are told
to pack
our crisscrossed packs
and line up in a single file.

Twenty at a time
board a motorboat
heading toward the dot.

An arm extends
to help us board,
an arm hairy with fuzz.

I touch it,
so real and long,
not knowing if I will
have another chance
to touch golden fuzz.

I pluck one hair.

Mother slaps my hand.
Brother Quang speaks quickly
in the language I must learn.

The fuzzy man laughs.

I'm grateful the boat
starts to rock,
so Mother hasn't
the composure
to scold me,
not just yet.

I roll my fuzzy souvenir
between my thumb and finger
and can't help
but smile.

May 26

Tent City

We have landed
on an island
called Guam,
which no one can pronounce
except Brother Quang,
who becomes
translator for all.

Many others arrived
before us
and are living
in green tents
and sleeping on cots.

We eat inside a huge tent
where Brother Vū
becomes head chef,
heating up cans of
beef and potatoes
tasting like salty vomit.

We eat only
canned fruit
in thick syrup,

and everyone wants extras
but we get only a cup.

Brother Vũ somehow
brings home
a huge can,
pumping it to work out
his arm muscles.

We eat
straight from the can
as I search for
cherries and grapes.

May 28

Life in Waiting

A routine starts
as soon as we settle
into our tent.

Camp workers
teach us English
mornings and afternoons.

Evenings we have to ourselves.

We watch movies outdoors
with images projected
onto a white sheet.
Brother Quang translates
into a microphone,
his voice sad and slow.

If it's a young cowboy
like Clint Eastwood,
everyone cheers.
If it's an old cowboy,
like John Wayne,
most of us boo
and go swimming.

The Disney cartoons
lure out the girls,
who always surround
Brother Vũ,
begging him to break
yet another piece of wood.

I can still hear them begging
when I go sit with Brother Khôi,
who rarely speaks anymore
but I'm happy to be near him.

June to early July

Nước Mắm

Someone
should be kissed
for having the heart
to send cases of fish sauce
to Guam.

Everything is
more edible
with *nước mắm*.

Brother Vũ
sautés the beef-and-potato goo
with onions
and sprinkles on the magic sauce
before serving the mess with rice.

Lines extend to the beach.

Someone catches
a sea creature
puffy and watery
like a cucumber.

Brother Vũ slices it
into slippery strips

and stews it with
seaweed
and the magic sauce.

So many appetites
wake up
that Brother Vũ
just has time
to cook rice
and serve it with
plain fish sauce.

People begin to cook
as long as they
can get a cup
of *nước mắm*.

Brother Khôi hands it out
in the same white cups
as tea.

Both dark brown,
so of course
I drink a gulp of the
most salty,
most bitter,
most fishy

tea
ever.

My head whirls
and my breath stinks
for days.

I do not mind.

July 1

Amethyst Ring

Mother wants to sell
the amethyst ring
Father brought back
from America,
where he trained
in the navy
before I was born.

She wants to buy
needles and thread,
fabric and sandals
from the camp's
black market.

I have never seen her
without this purple rock.
I can't fall asleep
unless I twist the ring
and count circles.

Brother Quang says,
NO!
What's the point of
new shirts and sandals

if you lose the last
tangible remnant of love?

I don't understand
what he said
but I agree.

July 2

Choose

Some choose to go to France
because many Vietnamese
moved there
when North and South
divided years ago.

Uncle Sơn says
come with his family
to Canada,
where his sister lives
and can help watch over us
until Father returns.

Mother knows his wife
would mind.
She tells him
Canada is too cold.

We stand in line
to fill out papers.
Every family must decide
by tonight,
when fireworks will explode
in honor of America's birth.

Mother starts to write
"Paris,"
home of a cousin
she has never met.

The man behind us whispers,
Choose America,
more opportunities there,
especially for a family
with boys ready to work.

Mother whispers back,
My sons
must first go to college.

If they're smart
America will give them
scholarships.

Mother chooses.

July 4

Another Tent City

We are flown
to another tent city
in humid, hot Florida,
where alligators are shown
as entertainment.

The people in charge
bring in Saigon-famous singers
to raise refugee spirits,
but faces keep twisting with worries.

For a family to leave,
an American must come to camp
and sponsor a family.

We wait and wait,
but Mother says a possible widow,
three boys, and a pouty girl
make too huge a family
by American standards.

A family of three
in the tent to our left
gets sponsored to Georgia;

the couple to our right
goes to South Carolina.

Newcomers leave before us.
Mother can barely eat,
while Brother Quang
picks the skin at his elbows.

I don't mind being here.
My hair is growing
as I've become dark and strong
from running and swimming.

Then by chance Mother learns
sponsors prefer those
whose applications say "Christians."

Just like that
Mother amends our faith,
saying all beliefs
are pretty much the same.

July to early August

Alabama

A man comes
who owns a store
that sells cars
and wants to train
one young man
to be a mechanic.

He keeps holding up
one finger
before picking Brother Quang,
whose studies in engineering
impress him.

Mother doesn't care
what the man
came looking for.

By the time
she is done
staring, blinking,
wiping away tears,
all without speaking English,

our entire family
has a sponsor
to Alabama.

August 7

Our Cowboy

Our sponsor
looks just like
an American should.

Tall and pig-bellied,
black cowboy hat,
tan cowboy boots,
cigar smoking,
teeth shining,
red in face,
golden in hair.

I love him
immediately
and imagine him
to be good-hearted and loud
and the owner of a horse.

August 8

PART III

Alabama

Unpack and Repack

We're giddy
when we
get off the airplane.

Our cowboy,
who never takes off
his tall, tall hat,
delivers us
to his huge house,
where grass
spreads out so green
it looks painted.

Stay until you feel ready.

We smile
and unpack
the two outfits
we each own.

One look at
our cowboy's wife,
arms, lips, eyes
contorted into knots,
and we repack.

August 15

English Above All

We sit and sleep in the lowest level
of our cowboy's house,
where we never see
the wife.

I must stand on a chair
that stands on a tea table
to see
the sun and the moon
out a too-high window.

The wife insists
we keep out of
her neighbors' eyes.

Mother shrugs.
More room here
than two mats on a ship.

I wish she wouldn't try
to make something bad
better.

She calls a family meeting.

Until you children
master English,
you must think, do, wish
for nothing else.
Not your father,
not our old home,
not your old friends,
not our future.

She tries to mean it
about Father,
but I know at times
words are just words.

August 16

First Rule

Brother Quang says
add an *s* to nouns
to mean more than one
even if there's
already an *s*
sitting there.

Glass
Glass-es

All day
I practice
squeezing hisses
through my teeth.

Whoever invented
English
must have loved
snakes.

August 17

American Chicken

Most food
our cowboy brings
is wrapped in plastic
or pushed into cans,
while chicken and beef
are chopped and frozen.

We live on
rice, soy sauce,
canned corn.

Today our cowboy brings
a paper bucket of chicken,
skin crispy and golden,
smelling of perfection.

Brother Khôi recoils,
vowing to never eat
anything with wings.

Our cowboy bites on a leg,
grins to show teeth and gums.

I wonder if he's so friendly
because his wife is so mean.

We bite.

The skin tastes as promised,
crunchy and salty,
hot and spicy.

But
Mother wipes
the corners of her mouth
before passing her piece
into her napkin.

Brother Vũ gags.

Our cowboy scrunches
his brows,
surely thinking,
why are his refugees
so picky?

Brother Quang forces
a swallow
before explaining
we are used to
fresh-killed chicken
that roamed the yard

snacking on
grains and worms.

Such meat grows
tight in texture,
smelling of meadows
and tasting sweet.

I bite down on a thigh;
might as well bite down on
bread soaked in water.

Still,
I force yum-yum sounds.

I hope to ride
the horse our cowboy
surely has.

August 20

Out the Too-High Window

Green mats of grass
in front of every house.

Vast windows
in front of sealed curtains.

Cement lanes where
no one walks.

Big cars
pass not often.

Not a noise.

Clean, quiet
loneliness.

August 21

Second Rule

Add an *s* to verbs
acted by one person
in the present tense,
even if there's
already an *s* sound
nearby.

She choose-s
He refuse-s

I'm getting better
at hissing,
no longer spitting
on my forearms.

August 22

American Address

Our cowboy
in an even taller hat
finds us a house
on Princess Anne Road,
pays rent ahead
three months.

Mother could not believe
his generosity
until Brother Quang says
the American government
gives sponsors money.

Mother is even more amazed
by the generosity
of the American government
until Brother Quang says
it's to ease the guilt
of losing the war.

Mother's face crinkles
like paper on fire.
She tells Brother Quang
to clamp shut his mouth.

People living on
others' goodwill
cannot afford
political opinions.

I inspect our house.

Two bedrooms,
one for my brothers,
one for Mother and me.

A washing machine,
because no one here
will scrub laundry
in exchange for
a bowl of rice.

The stove spews out
clean blue flames,
unlike the ashy coals
back home.

What I love best:
the lotus-pod shower,
where heavy drops

will massage my scalp
as if I were standing
in a monsoon.

What I don't love:
pink sofas, green chairs,
plastic cover on a table,
stained mattresses,
old clothes,
unmatched dishes.

All from friends
of our cowboy.

Even at our poorest
we always had
beautiful furniture
and matching dishes.

Mother says be grateful.

I'm trying.

August 24

Letter Home

As soon as we have an address
Mother writes
all the way to the North
where Father's brother
anchors down the family line
in their ancestral home.

It's the first time
Mother has been allowed
to contact anyone in the North
since the country divided.

It'll be the first time
Father's brother
learns of his disappearance.

Unless,
Father has sent word
that he's safe
after all.

I shiver
with hope.

August 25

Third Rule

Always an exception.

Do *not* add an *s*
to certain nouns.

One deer,
two deer.

Why no *s* for two deer,
but an *s* for two monkeys?

Brother Quang says
no one knows.

So much for rules!

Whoever invented English
should be bitten
by a snake.

August 26

Passing Time

I study the dictionary
because grass and trees
do not grow faster
just because
I stare.

I look up

Jane: not listed

sees: to eyeball something

Spot: a stain

run: to move really fast

Meaning: _____ *eyeballs stain move.*

I throw the dictionary down
and ask Brother Quang.

Jane is a name,
not in the dictionary.

Spot is a common name
for a dog.

(Girl named) Jane sees (dog named) Spot run.

I can't read
a baby book.

Who will believe
I was reading
Nhất Linh?

But then,
who here knows
who he is?

August 27

Neigh Not Hee

Brother Quang
is tired of translating.
Our sponsor takes me
to register for school alone.

As my personal cowboy
for the day,
he will surely
let me ride his horse.

I start to climb
into his too-tall truck
but his two fingers
walk in the air.

This means
I'm to walk to school.

Turn right where flowers
big as dinner plates
grow strangely *blue*.

Turn left where
purple fluffy wands

arch on tall bushes
inviting butterflies.

Sweat beads plump up
on my cowboy's upper lip.
My armpits embarrass me.
I must remember
to not raise the reins high.

We walk and walk
on a road
where the horizon
keeps extending.

Finally,
we stop at
a fat, red
brick building.

Paperwork, paperwork
with a woman who
pats my head
while shaking her own.

I step back,
hating pity,

having learned
from Mother that
the pity giver
feels better,
never the pity receiver.

On the walk home
I take a deep breath,
forcing myself to say,
You, hor-ssssse?
Hee, hee, hee.
I go, go.

My personal cowboy
shakes his head.

I repeat myself
and gallop.

He scrunches his face.

I say, *Hor-ssssse*
and *Hee, hee, hee,*
until my throat hurts.

We get home.

Brother Quang
has to translate,
after all.

No, Mr. Johnston
doesn't have a horse,
nor has he ever ridden one.

What kind of a cowboy is he?

To make it worse,
the cowboy explains
horses here go
neigh, neigh, neigh,
not *hee, hee, hee.*

No they don't.

Where am I?

August 29

Fourth Rule

Some verbs
switch all over
just because.

I am
She is
They are
He was
They were

Would be simpler
if English
and life
were logical.

August 30

The Outside

Starting tomorrow
everyone must
leave the house.

Mother starts sewing
at a factory;
Brother Quang begins
repairing cars.

The rest of us
must go to school,
repeating the last grade,
left unfinished.

Brother Vũ wants
to be a cook
or teach martial arts,
not waste a year
as the oldest senior.

Mother says
one word:
College.

Brother Khôi
gets an old bicycle to ride,
but Mother says
I'm too young for one
even though I'm
a ten-year-old
in the fourth grade,
when everyone else
is nine.

Mother says,
*Worry instead
about getting sleep
because from now on
no more naps.
You will eat lunch
at school
with friends.*

What friends?

You'll make some.

What if I can't?

You will.

What will I eat?

What your friends eat.

But what will I eat?

Be surprised.

I hate surprises.

Be agreeable.

*Not without knowing
what I'm agreeing to.*

Mother sighs,
walking away.

September 1

Sadder Laugh

School!

I wake up with
dragonflies
zipping through
my gut.

I eat nothing.

I take each step toward school evenly,
trying to hold my stomach
steady.

It helps that
the morning air glides cool
like a constant washcloth
against my face.

Deep breaths.

I'm the first student in class.

My new teacher has brown curls
looped tight to her scalp
like circles in a beehive.

She points to her chest:
MiSSS SScott,
saying it three times,
each louder
with ever more spit.

I repeat, *MiSSS SScott*,
careful to hiss every *s*.

She doesn't seem impressed.

I tap my own chest:
Hà.

She must have heard
ha,
as in funny *ha-ha-ha*.

She fakes a laugh.

I repeat, *Hà*,
and wish I knew
enough English
to tell her
to listen for
the diacritical mark,

this one directing
the tone
downward.

My new teacher tilts
her head back,
fakes
an even sadder laugh.

September 2
Morning

Rainbow

I face the class.
MiSSS SScott speaks.
Each classmate says something.

I don't understand,
but I see.

Fire hair on skin dotted with spots.
Fuzzy dark hair on skin shiny as lacquer.
Hair the color of root on milky skin.
Lots of braids on milk chocolate.
White hair on a pink boy.
Honey hair with orange ribbons on see-through skin.
Hair with barrettes in all colors on bronze bread.

I'm the only
straight black hair
on olive skin.

September 2
Midmorning

Black and White and Yellow and Red

The bell rings.
Everyone stands.
I stand.

They line up;
so do I.

Down a hall.
Turn left.
Take a tray.
Receive food.
Sit.

On one side
of the bright, noisy room,
light skin.
Other side,
dark skin.

Both laughing, chewing,
as if it never occurred
to them
someone medium
would show up.

I don't know where to sit
any more than
I know how to eat
the pink sausage
snuggled inside bread
shaped like a corncob,
smeared with sauces
yellow and red.

I think
they are making fun
of the Vietnamese flag
until I remember
no one here likely knows
that flag's colors.

I put down the tray
and wait
in the hallway.

September 2
11:30 a.m.

144

Loud Outside

Another bell,
another line,
this time outside.

Every part
of the rainbow
surrounds me,
shouting, pushing.

A pink boy with white hair
on his head
and white eyebrows and
white eyelashes
pulls my arm hair.

Laughter.

It's true my arm hair
grows so long and black.

Maybe he is curious
about my long, black arm hair
like I was curious
about the golden fuzz

on the arm
of the rescue-ship sailor.

He pokes my cheek.

Howls from everyone.

He pokes my chest.

I see nothing but
squeezed eyes,
twisted mouths.

No,
they're not curious.

I want to pluck out every white hair
to see if the boy's scalp
matches the pink of his face.

I wish this
but walk away.

September 2
Afternoon

Laugh Back

The pink boy and two loud friends
follow me home.

I count each step
to walk faster.

I won't let them
see me run.

I count in English,
forcing it
to the front
of my mind.

I can't help but
glance back.

The pink boy shouts,
showing a black hole
where sharp teeth glow.

I walk faster,
count faster
in English.

Not that I care
to understand
what Pink Boy says,
but I have to
if I'm to laugh back
at him
one day.

September 2
After school

Quiet Inside

Brother Khôi is home,
not talking.

We sit together
shelling peanuts.
I keep my day inside.

Mother comes home
with two fingers
wrapped in white.
The electric machine
sews so fast.

Brother Quang comes home,
throws down his uniform shirt,
goes to the bathroom.
At dinner
his fingernails are still
rimmed in black oil.

Brother Vũ comes in
whistling.

He eats

two, three, four
pork chops.

I eat
one, two chops.

I have a feeling
having muscles
makes whistling
possible.

September 2
Evening

Fly Kick

I sneak into
my brothers' room.

The full moon shines on
the bulkiest lump.

I shake it awake.
Outside!

Brother Vũ swats my hand
but follows me.

Moonlight turns us silver.

They pulled my arm hair.
They threw rocks at me.
They promised to stomp on my chest.

Brother Vũ yawns.

A boy did pull my arm hair!

Brother Vũ pats my head.
Ignore him.

It's not like I follow him around.
Why were you whistling?

Someone called me Ching Chong.

Is that good?

Didn't sound good.
Then he tripped me,
so I flew up and
almost scissor-kicked him
in the face.

You missed?

I wanted him to stop,
not hurt him.
I didn't even like
seeing him scared.

I would have kicked him.
Teach me to fly-kick, please.

Not with your temper.

I shout, I'm so mad.
I shouldn't have to run away.

Tears come.

Brother Vũ
has always been afraid
of my tears.
I'll teach you defense.

How will that help me?

He smiles huge,
so certain of himself.
You'll see.

September 2
Late

Chin Nod

Next morning
halfway down the block,
away from Mother's eyes,
I hear the *clink clank*
of Brother Khôi's bicycle.

He stops and pats
the upper bar
of the triangle frame.

I sit sidesaddle,
holding on to the handlebar.
The edges of our hands
touch.

As we glide away
I ask,
Every day?

I feel his chin
nod into
the top of my head.

After school too?

Another chin nod.

We glide
and I feel as if
I'm floating.

September 3

Feel Dumb

MiSSS SScott
points to me,
then to the letters
of the English alphabet.

I say
A B C and so on.

She tells the class
to clap.

I frown.

MiSSS SScott
points to the numbers
along the wall.

I count up to twenty.

The class claps
on its own.

I'm furious,
unable to explain
I already learned

fractions
and how to purify
river water.

So this is
what dumb
feels like.

I hate, hate, hate it.

September 10

Wishes

I wish

Brother Khôi wouldn't
keep inside
how he endures
the hours in school,

that Mother wouldn't
hide her bleeding fingers,

that Brother Quang wouldn't
be so angry after work.

I wish

our cowboy could be persuaded
to buy a horse,

that I could be invisible
until I can talk back,

that English could be learned
without so many rules.

I wish

Father would appear
in my class
speaking beautiful English
as he does French and Chinese
and hold out his hand
for mine.

Mostly
I wish
I were
still
smart.

September 11

Hiding

Brother Vũ
now makes everyone
call him
Vu Lee,
a name I must say
without giggling
to get defense lessons.

I need the lessons.

I'm hiding in class
by staring at my shoes.

I'm hiding during lunch
in the bathroom,
eating hard rolls
saved from dinner.

I'm hiding during outside time
in the same bathroom.

I'm hiding after school
until Brother Khôi
rides up to
our secret corner.

With Vu Lee
I squat in
đứng tấn,
weight on legs,
back straight,
arms at my sides,
fingers relaxed,
eyes everywhere at once.

I'm practicing
to be seen.

Neighbors

Eggs explode
like smears of snot
on our front door.

Just dumb kids,
says our cowboy.

Bathroom paper hangs
like ghosts
from our willow.

More dumb kids,
says our cowboy.

A brick
shatters the front window,
landing on our dinner table
along with a note.

Brother Quang
refuses to translate.

Mother shakes her head
when Vu Lee pops his muscles.

Our cowboy
calls the police,
who tell us
to stay inside.

Hogwash,
our cowboy says,
then spits a brown blob
of tobacco.

I repeat, *Hogwash,*
puckering for the ending of
ssssshhhhhh.

Mother decides
we must meet
our neighbors.

Our cowboy leads,
giving us each a cowboy hat
to be tilted
while saying,
Good mornin'.

Only I wear the hat.

In the house

to our right
a bald man
closes his door.

Next to him
a woman
with yellow hair
slams hers.

Next to her
shouts reach us
behind a door unopened.

Redness crawls across
my brothers' faces.
Mother pats their backs.

Our cowboy leads us
to the house on our left.

An older woman
throws up her arms
and hugs us.

We're so startled
we stand like trees.

She points to her chest:
MiSSSisss WaSSShington.

She hugs our cowboy
and kisses him.

I thought only
husbands and wives
do that when alone.

We find out
MiSSSisss WaSSShington
is a widow and retired teacher.
She has no children
but has a dog named Lassie
and a garden that takes up
her backyard.

She volunteers
to tutor us all.

My time with her
will be right after school.

I'm afraid to tell her
how much help I'll need.

September 14

New Word a Day

MiSSSisss WaSShington
has her own rules.

She makes me memorize
one new word a day
and practice it
ten times in conversation.

For every new word
that sticks to my brain
she gives me
fruit in bite sizes, drowning in sweet, white fluff;
cookies with drops of chocolate small as rain;
flat, round, pan-fried cakes floating in syrup.

My vocabulary grows!

She makes me learn rules
I've never noticed,
like *a*, *an*, and *the*,
which act as little megaphones
to tell the world
whose English
is still secondhand.

The house is red.
But:
We live in a house.

A, an, and *the*
do not exist in Vietnamese
and we understand
each other just fine.

I pout,
but MiSSSisss WaSSHington says
every language has annoyances and illogical rules,
as well as sensible beauty.

She has an answer for everything,
just like Mother.

September 16

More Is Not Better

I now understand

when they make fun of my name,
yelling *ha-ha-ha* down the hall

when they ask if I eat dog meat,
barking and chewing and falling down laughing

when they wonder if I lived in the jungle with tigers,
growling and stalking on all fours.

I understand
because Brother Khôi
nodded into my head
on the bike ride home
when I asked if kids
said the same things
at his school.

I understand
and wish
I could go back
to not understanding.

September 19

HA LE LU DA

Our cowboy says
our neighbors
would be more like neighbors
if we agree to something
at the Del Ray Southern Baptist Church.

I've seen the church name
on a sign
where blaring yellow sun rays
spell GOD.

Our cowboy and his wife
wait for us
in the very first row.
He's smiling;
she's not.

A plump man
runs onto the stage
SHOUTING.

Everyone except us
greets him,
HA LE LU DA.

The more he SHOUTS,
the more everyone sings
HA LE LU DA.

Later a woman
smelling of honeysuckle
signals for all of us to follow.

Mother and I are told
to change into
shapeless white gowns.

We line up in a hallway
too bright and too bare,
where my brothers await us
frowning,
all wearing the same
shapeless white gowns.

I giggle.
Mother pinches me
then steps forward first.

The plump man
waits for her
in a tiny pool.
One hand holds her nose,

another hand on her back,
pushing her *under*.

I start to jump into the pool,
but Mother is standing again,
coughing,
hair matted to her face,
eyes narrowing
at me.

Each of my brothers
gets dipped.

My turn comes,
no matter how
I laser-eye Mother
to stop it.

And yet
it's not over.

We must get dressed
and line up onstage
next to the plump man,
our cowboy,
and his smiling wife.
Her lips curl up even more

as people line up
to kiss our cheeks.

Drops from wet hair
drip down my back.

Bumps enlarge on
my chilled skin
as I realize
we will be coming back
every Sunday.

September 21

Can't Help

Mother taps her nails
on the dining table,
her signal for solitude
to chant.

I shuffle off to our room
but am still with her
through my ears.

She chants,
Nam Mô A Di Đà Phật
Nam Mô Quan Thế Âm Bồ Tát

Such quiet tones
after a day of
shouts and HA LE LU DAs.

Clang clang clang,
a spoon chimes
against a glass bowl.

Nothing like
clear-stream bell echoes
from a brass gong.

Instead of jasmine incense,
Mother burns dried orange peels.
Ashy bitter citrus
invades our room.

Nothing like
the floral wafts
that once calmed me.

I try
but can't fall sleep,
needing amethyst-ring twirls
and her lavender scent.

I'm not as good as Mother
at making do.

Finally she comes in
and turns from me,
her signal for more
time alone.

I lie frozen,
sniffing for
traces of lavender.

Too faint
yet I dare not roll closer.

She sighs,
extends it
into a sniffle.

Where are you?
Should we keep hoping?

She thinks
I am asleep.

More sniffles,
so gentle
I would miss them
by inhaling too deeply.

Come home,
come home and see how
our children have grown.

All my life
I've wondered
what it's like
to know someone

for forever
then *poof*
he's gone.

Another sigh.

*It's more difficult here
than I imagined.*

I thought so,
despite her own rule
Mother can't help
yearning for Father
any more than I can help
tasting ripe papaya
in my sleep.

*September 21
Late*

Spelling Rules

Sometimes
the spelling changes
when adding an *s*.

Knife becomes *knives*.

Sometimes
a *c* is used
instead of a *k*,
even if
it makes more sense
for *cat* to be spelled *kat*.

Sometimes
a *y* is used
instead of an *e*,
even if
it makes more sense
for *moldy* to be spelled *molde*.

Whoever invented English
should have learned
to spell.

September 30

Cowboy's Gifts

Our cowboy likes
to bring us gifts.

The breathing catfish
was Mother's favorite.

I couldn't watch Vu Lee
kill and clean it,
but it tasted so good.

After getting us dipped at church,
our cowboy brought gifts
even more often.

Vu Lee always asks for beef jerky,
pointing to his muscles.

I prefer really fat grapes.

Today our cowboy brings
chips and chocolate.

My brothers and I
finish the chips
in a flash.

Later Mother
throws away
what's left of the candy.

After she falls asleep,
I retrieve the bars.

They'll be better
than hard rolls
for lunch.

October 4

Someone Knows

My word for today
is *delicious*,
dì lít-sì-ishss.

MiSSSisss WaSSShington asks,
Was your lunch delicious?

Before speaking,
I have to translate
in my head.

She waits.

I eat candy in toilet.

MiSSSisss WaSSShington
looks panicked.
WHAT?

I realize my mistake.
Oh, the *toilet.*

She doesn't look
any happier.

I add,
Not candy all time.

But you always *eat in the bathroom?*

I nod.

Why?

How can I explain
dragonflies do somersaults
in my stomach
whenever I think of
the noisy room
full of mouths
chewing and laughing?

I'm still translating
when her eyes get red.

*I'll pack you a lunch
and you can eat at your desk.*

No eat in class.

I'll fix that.

Things will get better,
just you wait.

I don't believe her
but it feels good
that someone knows.

Most Relieved Day

At lunch the next day
I stay in class.

MiSSS SScott nods.

Can it be this easy?

Inside my first
brown paper bag:
a white meat sandwich,
an apple,
crunchy curly things
sprinkled with salt,
and a cookie dotted
with chocolate raindrops.

Something salty,
something sweet,
perfect.

I hear pounding footsteps
in the long hall.

I stop chewing.

Two students
run into class,
giggling.

I firm my muscles,
ready for the giggles
to explode into laughter
thrown at me.

But smiles appear instead.

The girl has
red hair swaying to her bottom,
a skirt falling to her calves.

She says, *Pam*. I hear *Pem*.

The boy of coconut-shell skin
is dressed
better than for church,
a purple bow tie,
a white white shirt
that wouldn't wrinkle
even if he rolled down a hill.

His shaved head

is so shiny and perfect
I want to touch it.

He speaks slowly and loudly,
but I don't mind
because he's still smiling.

He says, *Steven*.
I hear *SSsi-Ti-Vân*.

I have not
seen them in class.
But then, I mostly
stare at my shoes.

I will write in my journal
October 14 is
Most Relieved Day,
as I have noted
April 30 was
Saigon Is Gone Day
and September 2 was
Longest Day *Ever*.

Though I was saving
Most Relieved Day

for Father's return,
he can have the title:
My Life's Best Day.

October 14

Smart Again

Pink Boy
stands at the board.

He can't multiply
18 by 42.

I go to the board,
chalk the answer
in five moves.

My cheekbones lift
to the ceiling
until I see horror
on the faces
of Pem and SSsì-Ti-Vân.

Pink Boy is glowing red
against white hair,
white eyebrows,
and white eyelashes.

MiSSS SScott
nudges me toward my seat.

Pem reaches for my hand,
hers trembling.

I know
Pink Boy will get me,
but right now
I feel smart.

October 20

Hair

One day
the honey-hair girl
takes her pink ribbons
and knots pigtails in my hair.

She stares,
shakes her head,
yanks back her ribbons.
Pink don't look good on you.

Then three girls
of bronze-bread skin
remove colorful barrettes
from their hair
and twist onto my head
so many braids.

The girls' hair holds
the shape of braids
even without barrettes.

Pem and SSsì-Ti-Vân nod,
so I keep still.

Walking home,
my shadow shows
eels dancing on my head
with tails in shapes of
bows, stars, hearts.

Mother and Brothers
notice,
pause,
then go on with their day.

It isn't easy
to sleep on a pile of
plastic barrettes.

The next morning
when the girls
slip off the barrettes,
my hair falls back
to being straight.

The girls
yank my flat strands,
walk away.

I've spent my life
wishing for long hair
and this is what I get.

October 23

The Busy One

Vu Lee no longer
has time for just me.

At sunrise
he throws newspapers
onto porches.

After school
he flips perfect circles
of beef.

At sunset
he teaches Bruce Lee moves
in our front yard.

We line up in five rows,
squatting and shifting,
the only moves
he has taught us.

I make sure to get
in the front row.

First came
the eager boys.

Next came
the giggly girls.
Then came
our neighbors who
couldn't help their curiosity.

They wave back now,
at times bringing
jiggly, colorful food
we don't eat.

Everyone in Vu Lee's class
wears yellow.
Some even bought suits
exactly like Bruce Lee's.

Brothers Quang and Khôi join too.

Once I saw Mother
behind the curtains,
smiling.

I squatted low and sturdy then.

October 28

War and Peace

MiSSS SScott
shows the class
photographs

of a burned, naked girl
running, crying
down a dirt road

of people climbing, screaming,
desperate to get on
the last helicopter
out of Saigon

of skeletal refugees,
crammed aboard a
sinking fishing boat,
reaching up to the heavens
for help

of mounds of combat boots
abandoned by soldiers
of the losing side.

She's telling the class
where I'm from.

She should have shown
something about
papayas and Tết.

No one would believe me
but at times
I would choose
wartime in Saigon
over
peacetime in Alabama.

October 29

Pancake Face

Pem is dressed
in a skirt to the floor
like the pioneers
in our textbook.

SSsì-Ti-Vân
wears a beard
like President Lincoln.

I didn't know
today is pretend day.

Pink Boy keeps asking,
What are you?

By the end of school
he yells an answer:
She should be a pancake.
She has a pancake face.

It doesn't make sense
until
it does.

I run,
hearing laughter
loud loud loud,
which still echoes when Mother comes home.

I can't keep the day inside anymore.

Mother asks,
What's a pancake?

Tears gush
because I can't
make myself explain
a pancake
is
very
very
flat.

October 31
Halloween

Mother's Response

Mother strokes my head.

Chant, my child,
Breathe in, peaceful mind.
Breathe out, peaceful smile.

She strokes my back.

Chant, my daughter;
your whispers will bloom
and shelter you
from words
you need not hear.

Chant
Nam Mô A Di Đà Phật
Nam Mô Quan Thế Âm Bồ Tát.

She strokes my arm.

I chant,
wanting the gentle strokes
to continue forever.

I chant,
wanting Mother's calmness
to sink into me.

October 31
Night

MiSSSisss WaSShington's Response

I'm quiet
during my lesson
with MiSSSisss WaSShington.

For a long time
I stare at the floral wallpaper
and shelves full of books,
then I notice
a framed photograph
of a boy in uniform.

I had not known of her son Tom
or of his death as a
twenty-year-old soldier
in the very place
where I was born.

I never thought
the name of my country
could sound so sad.

I'm afraid to look
at MiSSSisss WaSShington.
You hate me?

Child, child.

She comes close
and hugs me.

Right then I tell her
about the pancake.

She hugs me tighter,
then pulls out a book.

A book of photographs:
a dragon dance at Tết,
schoolgirls in white *áo dàis*,
a temple built on a tree trunk.

Tom had sent home
these photographs
of a hot, green country
that he loved and hated
just the same.

I suck in breath:
a photograph of
a papaya tree
swaying broad,
fanlike leaves

in the full sun,
showing off a bundle
of fat orange piglets.

Excited, I yell,
Đu đủ!
I'm stabbing at the image.
Best food.

Papaya?
Your favorite food is papaya?

By the time I teach her
đu đủ
and she teaches me
doo-doo
we're laughing so hard
we're hungry for pancakes.

She tells me
to take
the book home.

November 3

Cowboy's Response

Before school
our cowboy shows up.
MiSSSisss WaSShington told him
about the pancake.

He whispers to Mother and Brother Quang.
All will escort me to school
with MiSSSisss WaSShington.

I do not feel good.

In the principal's office
sit Pink Boy and his mother.

It's very hot in here.

Lots of strained voices
holding in anger.

Finally all eyes
are on Pink Boy,
who wrestles out, *Sorry*.

I feel like throwing up.

Mother rescues him:
We know you're from a proper family
and did not realize
the damage of your insult.

While Brother Quang translates,
Pink Boy's eyes let me know
he hates me even more.

November 5

Boo-Da, Boo-Da

MiSSS SScott
shows photographs
of the S shape
of Vietnam,
of green mountains and long beaches,
of a statue of the Buddha reclining.

She asks me,
Would you like to say anything?

I know Buddha.

I hear laughter
and a murmur building:
Boo-Da, Boo-Da.

MiSSS SScott hushes them.

All day I hear whispers:
Boo-Da, Boo-Da.

I watch the clock,
listen for the final bell,
and dash.

Pink Boy and friends follow,
releasing shouts of
Boo-Da, Boo-Da
as I put one leg
in front of the other
faster
faster
but not fast enough
to not hear them
scream
Boo-Da, Boo-Da.

I turn down
the wrong street,
away from the corner
where Brother Khôi would be.

I have no choice
but to *run*.

I turn right where purple flowers
curve like baby moons
over butterfly bushes.

Footsteps pound
right behind me.

Turn left where flowers grow *blue*.

I wish I could control it,
but the plates of flowers
are now blue smears
from my near tears.

Boo-Da, Boo-Da
breathes into the back
of my neck.

Faster, faster.
My legs try,
but the shouts are upon me.

Someone pulls my hair,
forcing me to turn
and see
a black hole in a pink face:
Boo-Da, Boo-Da Girl.

My palms cover my eyes.

I run.

All the while
surging from my gut:

fire
sourness
weight
anger
loneliness
confusion
embarrassment
shame.

November 7

Hate It

I don't make it inside the house,
but sit
under the willow tree,
dig a hole
and into it
scream scream scream

I hate everyone!!!!

A lion's paw rips up my throat,
still I scream

I hate everyone!!!!

Hands grip my shoulders.

MiSSSisss WaSSShington
is on her knees.

Child, child, come with me.

I hate everyone!!!!

She hoists me up
by my armpits

and drags me across
the yard.

You poor child,
tell me, tell me.

It hurts too much
to keep screaming,
but it feels good
to thrash about
like a captured lizard.

Inside her house,
MiSSSisss WaSShington throws
her body on mine.

Hush, hush,
hush, hush.

She says it over and over
like a chant,
slowly.
Slowly
the screams that never stopped
inside my head
cool to a real whisper.

I hate everyone!

Even your mama?

She crosses her eyes,
puckers her lips.

I stop myself from laughing.

She pats my hand.

That one gesture
dissolves the last
of my hate spell.

November 7
After school

Brother Quang's Turn

Brother Quang comes home
with happy shouts.

He did it,
repairing a car
no one else could.

From now on
he's to work
only on engines.

Mother smiles so hard
she cries.

I pout.

When is it going to be
my turn?

November 12

Confessions

It's time to tell Mother
why misery
keeps pouncing on me.

I used to buy less pork
so I could buy fried dough.

I know.

You do?

What else?

I used to like making the girl
who shared my desk cry.

She tilts her head.

I know, Mother, I know, very bad.

She nods.

Now they make me cry.
Will I be punished forever?

Forever is quite long.

There's more;
it's really bad.

She lifts an eyebrow.

At dawn on Tết
I tapped my big toe
to the tile floor
first.

She widens her eyes.

I hate being told I can't do something because I'm a girl!

She doesn't scold me,
just nods.

Did I ruin the luck
of the whole family?
Is that why we're here?

My child,
how you shoulder the world!

I was superstitious,
that's all.
If anything,
you gave us luck
because we got out
and we're here.

Lucky
to be here?

Just wait,
you'll see.

I don't want to wait.
It's awful now.

Is it really so unbearable?

They chase me.
They yell "Boo-Da, Boo-Da" at me.
They pull my arm hair.
They call me Pancake Face.
They clap at me in class.
And you want me to wait?
Can I hit them?

Oh, my daughter,
at times you have to fight,
but preferably
not with your fists.

November 14

NOW!

Brother Quang takes us
to the grocery store.
Mother buys everything
to make egg rolls
for a coming holiday
when Americans eat a turkey
the size of a baby.

She has me ask the butcher,
Please grind our pork.

I'm sure I said it right,
but the butcher
sharpens his face,
slams down our meat,
and motions us away.

Mother wrinkles her brows,
thinking, pausing,
then rings the buzzer again.

Please, she says.
It comes out, *Peezzz.*

The butcher turns away
without a word.

Mother presses the buzzer
for a long time.

When the butcher returns,
he hears a lot of Vietnamese
in a voice stern and steady,
from eyes even more so.

Mother ends with a clear, *NOW!*

The butcher stares
then takes our meat
to the grinder.

November 22

Đu Đủ Face

Again they're yelling,
Boo-Da, Boo-Da,
but I know to run
toward Brother Khôi
two corners away.

Enough time
for them to repeat
hundreds of *Boo-Da*s.

Enough time
for me to turn and yell,
Gee-sus, Gee-sus.

I love how they stop,
mouths open.

My heart lifting,
I run and shout,
Bully!
Coward!
Pink Snot Face!

Words I learned from them
on the playground.

I turn to see
Pink Boy coming
close to me.

No longer pink,
he's red,
blood-orange red
like a ripe papaya.

Đu Đủ *Face!*

It's not my fault
if his friends hear
Doo-doo Face
and are laughing
right at him.

Brother Khôi is waiting.
I jump on.

December 4

Rumor

Friday

SSsì-Ti-Vân heard it from Pem
who heard it from the honey-hair girl
who heard it from the dot-on-face girl
who heard it from the white-hair boy
who heard it from all three girls in braids

that

Pink Boy

has gotten his sixth-grade cousin,
a girl two heads taller than the tallest of us,
with arm muscles that run up and down like mice,

to agree

to beat me up

when we come back

Monday.

December 5

221

A Plan

I don't have to tell Brother Khôi,
who heard in the halls
of *his* school
that my face
is to be flattened
flatter
tomorrow.

You don't have a flat face,
he says.
Besides, I have a plan.

December 7

Run

Five minutes
till the last bell
I lean toward the door,
legs bouncing,
books left on the floor.

Rrriiinnggg

I run,
Pem and SSsì-Ti-Vân
close behind.

Outside
Pem and I exchange
coats with hoods.

Pem heads down
my usual path.
I zip to the left.

SSsì-Ti-Vân stays
to block the door.

Running so fast,
I fly above the sidewalk.

Alone.

They must all be with Pem.

I stop at the new corner
where Brother Khôi said to wait.

Where is he?

Footsteps explode
from the street
that smacks into mine.

Pink Boy!

December 8
3:36 p.m.

A Shift

Pink Boy plows
toward me.

I squat in *đứng tấn*,
facing him.

His right arm extends
in a fist.

When he's close enough
for me to see
the white arm hair,
I shift my upper body
to the left,
legs sturdy,
eyes on the blur
that flies past me.

A *thud*.

Pink Boy writhes on the pavement.

I thought I would love
seeing him in pain.

But
he looks
more defeated than weak,
more helpless than scared,
liked a caged puppy.

He's getting up.

If I were to kick him,
it must be
now.

December 8
3:38 p.m.

WOW!

A roar.

Pink Boy and I
turn.

A gigantic motorcycle.

The rider in all black
stops.

The helmet comes off.

VU LEE!

WOW!

Pink Boy disappears.

Brother Khôi runs up,
out of breath,
pushing a bicycle
with a flat.

Vu Lee flicks his head.

I climb on first,
wrap my arms around a waist
tight as rope.
Brother Khôi climbs on next,
one hand holding
the handlebar of his bike.

We fly home.

December 8
3:43 p.m.

The Vu Lee Effect

Vu Lee
now picks me up
after school.

So
someone is always
saving lunch seats
for me, Pem, and SSsì-Ti-Vân;

someone is always
inviting us
to a party;

someone is always
hoping Vu Lee
will offer her a ride,
as he did
the huge cousin,
who now not only smiles
but waves at us.

Pink Boy
avoids us,
and we're glad.

December 16

Early Christmas

Mother invites our cowboy
and MiSSSisss WaSShington
for egg rolls.

They brought gifts,
not saying
Early Christmas,
not wanting
to embarrass us
for not having anything
to exchange.

From our cowboy
to Mother: two just-caught catfish
to Brother Quang: tuition for night college
to Vu Lee: jerky in ten flavors
to Brother Khôi: two fighting fish in separate jars
to me: a new coat

We laugh and say,
Perfect!

From MiSSSisss WaSShington
to Mother: a gong and jasmine incense
to Brother Quang: an engineering textbook

to Vu Lee: jerky in ten flavors
to Brother Khôi: a hamster
to me: three packages of something orange and dried

My family claps and says,
Perfect!

I frown.

December 20

Not the Same

Three pouches of
dried papaya

Chewy
Sugary
Waxy
Sticky

Not the same
at all.

So mad,
I throw all in the trash.

December 20
Night

But Not Bad

Mother slaps my hand.
Learn to compromise.

I refuse to retrieve the pouches,
pout,
go to bed,
stare at the photograph of a real papaya tree,
wonder if I'll ever taste sweet, tender, orange flesh
again.

GOOONNNNGGGGG
rings out;
how soothing a real gong sounds.

Swirls of incense
reach me,
hovering like a blanket,
tugging me in.

I wake up at faint light,
guilt heavy on my chest.

I head toward the trash can.

Yet
on the dining table
on a plate
sit strips of papaya
gooey and damp,
having been soaked in hot water.

The sugar has melted off
leaving
plump
moist
chewy
bites.

Hummm . . .

Not the same,
but not bad
at all.

December 20–21

PART IV

From Now On

Letter from the North

Eight months ago,
    war ended.
Four months ago,
    Mother sent our letter.
Today,
    Father's brother answers.

Still, we know nothing more.

Our uncle even went south
to talk with our old neighbors,
to find Father's old friends.

He consulted,
left word,
waited
until it became obvious
he would know nothing more.

His letter
doesn't tell us
what to do
from now on.

We look to Mother.

She doesn't tell us either.

Ours is a silent
Christmas Eve.

December 24

Gift-Exchange Day

Pem comes over
on gift-exchange day
with a doll
to replace
the mouse-bitten one
I told her about.

I almost scream
because the doll
with long black hair
is so beautiful.

But I whisper,
Thank you.

My high emotions
are squished beneath
the embarrassment
of not having a gift
for her.

December 25

What If

Brother Quang asks
what if
Father escaped to Cambodia
and is building an army
to go back and change history?

Vu Lee asks
what if
Father escaped to France
but can't remember his own history,
so he builds a new family
and is happy?

Brother Khôi asks
what if
Father escaped to Tibet
after shaving his head
and joining a monastery?

I can't think of anything
but can't let my brothers best me,
so I blurt out,
What if
Father is really gone?

From the sad look
on their faces
I know
despite their brave guesses
they have begun to accept
what I said on a whim.

December 29

A Sign

Mother says nothing
about Father

but

she chants every night,

long chants
where her voice
wavers between
hope and acceptance.

She's waiting
for a sign.

I'll decide
what she decides.

December 30

No More

First day back
after Christmas break,
I know I'm supposed
to wear everything new.

I don't have
anything new
except for the coat,
and a hand-me-down dress
still wrapped in plastic.

It's beige with blue flowers
made from a fabric fuzzy and thick,
perfect for this cold day.

Best of all
it's past my knees,
perfect for a cold bike ride.

Pem is wearing a new skirt
falling to her calves, as always.

SSsì-Ti-Vân's new white shirt
looks stiff as a wall.

As soon as I remove my coat,
everyone stops talking.

A girl in red velvet
comes over to me.
*Don't ya know flannel
is for nightgowns and sheets?*

I panic.

Pem shrugs.
*I can't wear pants
or cut my hair
or wear skirts above my calves;
what do I care what you wear?*

SSsì-Ti-Vân says,
It looks like a dress to me.

The red-velvet girl
points to the middle
of my chest.
*See this flower?
They only put that
on nightgowns.*

I look down
at the tiny blue flower
barely stitched on.

I rip it off.
Nightgown no more.

January 5

Seeds

I wear the same dress
to sleep,
telling Mother why.

I pretended not to care,
then no one cared,
so I really didn't care.

Mother laughs.

I tell her
a much worse embarrassment
is not having
a gift for Pem.

Mother nods, thinks,
goes to her top drawer.

I was saving this for you
for Tết,
but why wait?

In her palm lies
the tin of flower seeds
I had gathered with TiTi.

Perfect for Pem!

Mother always
thinks of everything.

January 5
Night

Gone

Mother runs in after work,
hands clenched into white balls,
words chopped into grunts,
face of ash.

We stare at her left hand.

The amethyst stone is gone!

Brother Quang drives us back
to the sewing factory
in his car made of mismatched parts.

We search where Mother sat,
then retrace her steps
to the cafeteria
to the bathroom
to the parking lot.

We repeat so often we lose count,
propelled by Mother's
wild eyes and
pressed mouth,
frightened of what

her expression would be
if . . .

At dusk,
the guards shoo us out.

We're afraid to look at Mother.

January 14

Truly Gone

When home,
Mother
retreats to our room,
misses dinner,
remains soundless.

At bedtime
we hear
the gong,
then chanting.

The chant is long,
the voice
low and sure.

Finally
she appears,
looks at each of us.

Your father is
truly gone.

January 14
Late

Eternal Peace

Mother wears
her brown *áo dài*
brought from home.

Each of my brothers
wears a suit,
too small or too big.

I wear a pink dress
of ruffles and lace,
which I hate,
but at least
it's definitely a dress.

Each of us faces the altar,
holding a lit incense stick
between palms in prayer.

Father's portrait
stares back.

This is as old
as we'll ever know him.

That thought
turns my eyes
red.

Mother says,
We'll chant
for Father's safe passage
toward eternal peace,
where his parents await him.

She pauses,
voice choked.

Father won't leave
if we hold on to him.
If you feel like crying,
think
at least now
we know.

At least
we no longer live
in waiting.

January 17

Start Over

I'm trying to tell
MiSSSisss WaSShington
about our ceremony for Father.

But it takes time to
match every noun and verb,
sort all the tenses,
remember all the articles,
set the tone for every *s*.

MiSSSisss WaSShington says
if every learner waits
to speak perfectly,
no one would learn
a new language.

Being stubborn
won't make you fluent.
Practicing will!
The more mistakes you make,
the more you'll learn not to.

They laugh.

Shame on them!
Challenge them to say
something in Vietnamese
and laugh right back.

I tell her
Father is at peace.

I tell her
I'd like to plant
flowers from Vietnam
in her backyard.

I tell her
Tết is coming
and luck starts over
every new year.

January 19

An Engineer, a Chef, a Vet, and Not a Lawyer

Brother Quang
has started night school
to restudy engineering
to become what
he was meant to be.

Mother smiles.

Vu Lee
refuses to apply to a real college,
instead will go to a cooking school
in San-fran-cis-co,
where his idol once walked.

Mother sighs,
twists her brows
to no effect.

Brother Khôi
announces he will become a doctor
of animals.

Mother starts to say something,
then nods.

Mother has always wanted
an engineer, a real doctor, a poet,
and a lawyer.

She turns to me.
You love to argue, right?

No I don't.

She brightens.

I vow to become
much more agreeable.

January 29

1976: Year of the Dragon

This Tết
there's no I Ching Teller of Fate,
so Mother predicts our year.

Our lives
will twist and twist,
intermingling the old and the new
until it doesn't matter
which is which.

This Tết
there's no *bánh chưng*
in the shape of a square,
made of pork,
glutinous rice,
and mung beans,
wrapped in banana leaves.

Mother makes her own
in the shape of a log,
made of pork,
regular rice,
and black beans,
wrapped in cloth.

Not the same,
but not bad.

As with every Tết
we are expected to

smile until it hurts
all three first days
of the year,

wear all new clothes
especially underneath,

not sweep,
not splash water,
not talk back,
not pout.

Mother thinks of everything.

She even asked Brother Quang
to bless the house
right after midnight,
so I couldn't beat him to it
by touching my big toe
to the carpet before dawn.

Mother has set up
an altar
on the highest bookshelf.

The same, forever-young
portrait of Father.

I have to look away.

We each hold an incense stick
and wait for the gong.

I pray for
Father to find warmth in his new home,
Mother to keep smiling more,
Brother Quang to enjoy his studies,
Vu Lee to drive me from and *to* school,
Brother Khôi to hatch an American chick.

I open my eyes.
The others are still praying.

What could they be asking for?

I think and think
then close my eyes again.
This year I hope

I truly learn
to fly-kick,
not to kick anyone
so much as
to fly.

Acknowledgments

Much thanks to Angie Wojak, Joe Hosking, Sarah Sevier, Tara Weikum, Rosemary Stimola, and of course my family (Mợ, Chị Mai, Anh Anh, Anh Tuấn, Anh Nam, Anh Zũng, Anh Tiến, Anh Sơn, Chị Hương), with whom I shared April 30, 1975, and weeks on a ship, events that decades later led me to Henri and An.

Inside Out & Back Again

BONUS MATERIAL

• Author's Note •

• Back Again: An interview with Thanhhà Lại •

• Telling Your Story: An activity for you and your family •

• Writing Poetry: Tips from Thanhhà Lại •

• Discussion Questions •

Author's Note

Dear Reader:

Much of what happened to Hà, the main character in *Inside Out & Back Again*, also happened to me.

At age ten, I, too, witnessed the end of the Vietnam War and fled to Alabama with my family. I, too, had a father who was missing in action. I also had to learn English and even had my arm hair pulled the first day of school. The fourth graders wanted to make sure I was real, not an image they had seen on TV. So many details in this story were inspired by my own memories.

Aside from remembering facts, I worked hard to capture Hà's emotional life. What was it like to live where bombs exploded every night yet where sweet snacks popped up at every corner? What was it like to sit on a ship heading toward hope? What was it like to go from knowing you're smart to feeling dumb all the time?

The emotional aspect is important because of something I noticed in my nieces and nephews. They may know in general where their parents came from, but they can't really imagine the noises and smells of Vietnam, the daily challenges of starting over in a strange land. I extend this idea to all: How much do we know about those around us?

I hope you enjoy reading about Hà as much as I have enjoyed remembering the pivotal year in my life. I also hope after you finish this book that you sit close to someone you love and implore that person to tell and tell and tell their story.

Thanhhà Lại

Back Again: An interview with Thanhhà Lại

From your Author's Note, we learn that Hà's tale isn't a complete work of fiction and that much of what happened to her happened to you. Why did you choose not to write a more biographical work? How are you and the character of Hà different?

I'm incapable of telling the truth. Somewhere, somehow, I always tend to embellish any memory, so I thought it was safe and best to tell my story as fiction with my real shadow hovering over the manuscript. The other factor has to do with my loud and huge family—there are nine children plus my mother. They were present for the duration of the story, so can you imagine what my email inbox would have looked like if I had attempted to tell my truth? Each sibling would have sent "corrections," so I took the quieter way out.

While Hà is based on myself, she is a spunkier version of me. I wasn't wishing to fly kick for any reason just a year after immigration. The process of rebuilding my corner of the world took more like a decade.

At one point in the story, Hà says that she would choose wartime in Saigon over peacetime in Alabama. Assuming you had similar feelings when you were her age, do you still feel this way today? How has growing up changed your outlook on the situation?

Hà had been in the United States for six months when she expressed a preference for wartime in Saigon over peacetime in Alabama. I did feel those sentiments, but it's been thirty-seven years since I landed in Montgomery. Whatever childhood slight happened to me, I should hope I have gotten over it by now.

Looking back, I don't blame fourth graders in Alabama for being perplexed by the first Asian they had seen outside of television. No doubt they transferred whatever was being said about the Vietnam War in 1975 onto me, not understanding that I was just a person, not a war.

Children do not act in a vacuum. How they behave directly reflects what adults are saying around them. So while I now understand my former classmates' behavior, I do expect them to have grown up and gained perspective and to speak with more care and insight around their own children. Refugees are still coming to the United States every day because elsewhere in the world wars still rage and people still flee. I choose to believe that these refugees would be greeted with more awareness and compassion than I was.

Inside Out & Back Again takes its title partly from one of the book's poems. Why did you decide on it for the title of your book? Did you ever have another title in mind?

While writing, I named my manuscript *Buddhists in Alabama,* and the title was so entrenched in my mind that when my editors asked for an alternative I was stumped. We brainstormed until my head hurt. At some point I think I typed *Inside Out,* and my editors suggested adding *& Back Again.*

Inside Out & Back Again is written in a style of poetry known as free verse. What made you decide to tell Hà's tale this way? Did you ever consider telling her story in prose?

I struggled for fifteen years to tell Hà's story in a voice that would be authentic. I tried long flowing sentences in third person, but that rang false because what distraught ten-year-old would think in long flowy sentences? Then I tried Hemingwayish close-third-person prose but that voice proved too distant to capture the character's rage. One day I just started jotting down exactly what Hà would be feeling, lonely and angry on the playground. The words came out in quick, sharp phrases that captured her feelings in crisp images. These phrases reflected what Vietnamese sounded like. Remember, Hà was thinking in Vietnamese because she hadn't learned English yet. Then I knew I would be able to penetrate her mind by writing in phrases choked with visuals.

Although you may not consider yourself a poet, do you have favorite poets or poems that you could share?

I've been reading Nguyễn Du's *Truyện Kiều (The Tale of Kiều)* for almost three decades. I'm in awe of how this master

Vietnamese poet can convey the world in six/eight syllable couplets. My favorite is: *Dẫu rằng sông cạn đá mòn, con tằm đến thác cũng còn vương tơ.* Loose translation: Even if rivers run dry and rocks are polished smooth, a silkworm upon death still emits silk. Meaning: A silkworm, the ultimate symbol for eternal love, displays proof of longing even in death.

I remember reading that couplet in my early twenties and my heart stopped. I thought how wonderful my life would be if I could spend hours conveying the world in as few words as possible. While writing *Inside Out & Back Again*, I got a taste of that life, and let me tell you, it was wonderful.

Even though Hà struggles to learn English in this story, she is an avid reader. Did you enjoy reading as much when you were a kid? What were some of your favorite books when you were growing up?

I read everything I could sneak from my siblings in Vietnam, but once here, with the shock of immigration and learning English, I stopped reading for pleasure. Instead I spent years memorizing a copy of the *American Heritage Dictionary* until the cover fell off. I only read what was required in English classes, and I still remember passages from S. E. Hinton novels and anything to do with animals, like *Old Yeller* and *Charlotte's Web*. My real discovery of fiction didn't happen until college. It began with a class called From Homer to Hemingway, and hasn't ended.

This story is bookended by Tết celebrations. In the first poem, Hà describes a tradition in which a male's foot must be the first to touch the ground on the first day of the New Year. This is said to bless the home and bring luck. Are there other traditions associated with this holiday?

Lots, I just couldn't fit them all in. One, the older family members give younger ones bright red envelopes stuffed with brand-new, crisp, good-luck money called *tiền lì xì*. My mom still gives me one every Tết, complete with a little poem on the envelope. I, in turn, give envelopes to my nieces, nephews, and daughter. Two, every house has a tangerine tree drooping with orange fruit to bring in luck. Three, every house has branches of peach blossoms or pots of yellow chrysanthemums to denote spring. Four, we snack on watermelon seeds dyed red, again to symbolize luck, and the trick calls for cracking a seed, splitting the shell, and pulling out the crunchy, white meat—all with your teeth. The streets are covered with red shells during this time. All of Vietnam shuts down for at least two weeks because most workers have gone home to their ancestral land. It's like celebrating New Year's, the December holidays, everybody's birthday, and the Fourth of July in one explosive bash.

Telling Your Story:
An activity for you and your family

Inside Out & Back Again tells the story of Hà and her family's journey from Saigon to America. The author decided the best way to tell this story was through poetry, but there are so many other ways to tell a story. What would be the best way for you to tell the story of your own family? Here are some suggestions that might help you find the perfect fit.

Family Tree—Whether you have a small family or a large one, a family tree is the perfect way to discover your roots, or where your family comes from. You may know who your grandparents are, but do you know who your grandparents' grandparents were? The farther back you go in your family's history, the more surprised you might be by what you find. Starting your own family tree might seem like a big task, but if you take it one step, or branch, at a time, your tree will be full before you know it.

Journal—Like Hà's poems in this book, a journal lets you record your day-to-day activities. Whether you write in it every day or once a month, it can help you chronicle the most important events in your family's history. Journals are an ongoing project, so you have to remember to keep writing in them. It's best to make a habit of it and pick a particular time of day, like before going to bed, so that you can sit down and compose an entry.

Scrapbook—Are you more of a visual person? Then scrapbooking might be just the right method for you to tell your story. Filled with photos to remember a celebration, ticket stubs to remember important games, artwork to remember a budding talent, or any number of other memorabilia, scrapbooks are filled with souvenirs from your past. Scrapbooking can be an ongoing activity or something you do once a year after you have collected numerous keepsakes.

Writing Poetry:
Tips from Thanhhà Lại

1. Use as few words as possible. First, write down your line. Then cut one word at a time while asking yourself, Has the meaning changed? If not, keep cutting. You want the syrup without any sap.

2. Conjure up fresh, concise images. Surprise the readers whenever possible. For example, instead of: "He killed the chicken," write: "A red line appeared across the hen's neck."

3. Say it without actually saying it. When conveying emotions, instead of outright saying, "She's sad (or happy)," employ an image or detail that reveals the character. Instead of: "She's sad he cut down her biggest papaya." Try: "Black seeds spill / like clusters of eyes / wet and crying."

Discussion Questions

1. Hà's story is told in a series of poems. What do you think about that? Find examples of different types of poems: For instance, find one that tells a story and another that paints a picture. Some of the poems have a specific date at the end, but others say "every day." Why do you think that is?

2. What did you know about Vietnamese culture before reading the story? What are some of the things you learned as you read?

3. Sometimes Hà is angry about being a girl. Why does she make sure to tap her big toe on the floor before her brothers wake up on the morning of the new year? When she thinks about that moment a year later, what does she say?

4. Why does Mother lock away the portrait of Father after chanting in the morning (p. 13)? What do you think you would do if you were Hà or one of her brothers and someone close to you passed away? What would you say to Mother?

5. What does Hà mean when she talks about "how the poor fill their children's bellies" (p. 37)? What is Mother trying to do when she talks about how lovely yam and manioc taste with rice? Why do you think Mother finally decides to leave Saigon?

6. Why does Hà love papaya so much? What might the fruit represent for her? How is that the same as or different from what the chick means for Brother Khôi?

7. On the ship, Hà touches the sailor's hairy arm and Mother slaps her hand away (p. 95). Why does Hà take a hair? How is her behavior on the ship similar to or different from that of the kids at school in Alabama when they notice Hà's features?

8. Hà describes her American town as "clean, quiet loneliness" (p. 122). How is life in Alabama different from Saigon? Describe each setting and the differences between the two. Are there any similarities?

9. What do you know about the cowboy who sponsors the family? Who do you think he is, and what are some reasons why you think he might have become a sponsor? What

about Mrs. Washington: Why might she have volunteered to be a teacher for Hà?

10. Hà says that the cowboy's wife insists they "keep out of her neighbors' eyes" (p. 116). Why would she do that? Why would neighbors slam their doors when Hà's family comes to say hello (p. 164)?

11. Why would sponsors prefer applications that say "Christians" (p. 108)? Do you agree with Hà's mother that "all beliefs are pretty much the same" (p. 108)? Do you think she did the right thing by saying that the family is Christian?

12. Why is it so important to Hà's mother that her children learn English? If your family moved to a foreign country right now, would you be eager to learn the language? Why, or why not?

13. Hà struggles to learn English and hates feeling stupid. She asks, "Who will believe I was reading Nhất Linh?" and then, "Who here knows who he is?" (p. 130). What do you think is behind her frustration? What does she want people to understand about her and her family?

14. Brother Quang says that Americans' generosity is "to ease the guilt of losing the war" (p. 124). What is he talking about? Why doesn't he take their generosity at face value?

15. What does Mother mean when she tells Hà to "learn to compromise" (p. 233)? Is she talking about dried papaya or something else? Give an example of a compromise that Mother has made.